BALL LIGHTNING

Written by

PAULY HART

GLOBE OF FIRE DESCENDING INTO A ROOM.

Spec Script

Seventh Draft 11/20/2025

Pauly Hart Art

PaulyHart.com

EmpiresAndGenerals@Gmail.com

Log Line:

When an 18-year-old Latina trapped reliving her birthday must watch her family die in an explosion over and over, she discovers the mysterious ball lightning that marked her birth holds the key to breaking the loop-if she can figure out what it wants from her before time runs out.

Published by Pauly Hart Art

Printed in the USA, where available.

ISBN: 978-1-955399-58-6

Cover Art: "Globe of Fire Descending into a Room" by Dr. G. Hartwig, London, 1886

For information about the author, please visit PaulyHart.com

Library of Congress Catalog Data is available at: Loc.gov

This book is available on Amazon.com

BALL LIGHTNING
A Screenplay by Pauly Hart

FADE IN:

EXT. HOSPITAL - NIGHT - FLASHBACK (18 YEARS AGO)
The sky is wrong. That's the first thing you notice. Storm
clouds roil purple and green, pregnant with something that
shouldn't be. Lightning cracks - not down, but SIDEWAYS -
dancing between clouds like it's looking for something.
SUPER: "San Francisco General Hospital - October 12th, 2006
- 12:33 PM"
INT. HOSPITAL DELIVERY ROOM - CONTINUOUS
Fluorescent lights flicker. A DOCTOR (40s, tired eyes)
checks monitors while a NURSE (50s, seen-it-all face)
adjusts equipment.
On the table: MARIA RODRIGUEZ (25), soaked in sweat,
gripping the rails hard enough her knuckles have gone
white. Her long black hair sticks to her face. She's
beautiful and terrified and strong all at once.

DOCTOR
(calm, practiced)

> Maria, the baby's breech. We're
> going to need you to push harder.
> Can you do that for me?

Maria nods, gasping. Outside the window, the storm
intensifies. The lights flicker again.

NURSE

> Doctor, her vitals are--

The monitors SCREECH. Everything goes haywire at once.

DOCTOR

> Get me--

A sound. Not thunder. Something else. Like the air itself
is screaming.
Through the window: A sphere of light. Ball lightning. The
size of a basketball, crackling with impossible colors -
blues and purples and whites that shouldn't exist together.
It floats there, hovering, LOOKING.
The Nurse backs away from the window, crossing herself.

NURSE
(whispered)

> Dios mio...

The ball lightning moves closer. The window doesn't stop
it. It passes through the glass like the glass isn't there.

DOCTOR

> What the--

MARIA
(screaming)

> The baby! The baby is coming!

The ball lightning hovers above Maria. It pulses. Once.
Twice. The lights in the room go supernova-bright, then--
DARKNESS.

The monitors flat-line. Complete silence.
Then: A baby's cry. Pure and strong.
The lights flicker back on. The ball lightning is gone. The
Doctor holds a newborn girl, covered in afterbirth and
GLOWING SLIGHTLY - no, that's just the lights stabilizing,
isn't it?

                    DOCTOR
              (shaken, but professional)
          It's a girl. She's... she's
          perfect.
He places the baby on Maria's chest. Maria, exhausted
beyond words, looks down at her daughter. The baby's eyes -
dark and impossibly aware - lock onto her mother's.

                    MARIA
              (whispered, trembling)
          Sofia. Her name is Sofia.
The Doctor checks his watch, makes a note.

                    DOCTOR
          Time of birth: 12:34 PM.
Through the window: The storm breaks. Sudden sunshine. The
sky, impossibly, is clear and blue.
The Nurse and Doctor exchange a look. Neither knows what to
say.

                    MARIA
              (to Sofia, soft)
          Especial y importante. You're
          going to be so special.
                                                  CUT TO:
INT. SOFIA'S BEDROOM - MORNING - PRESENT DAY
SUPER: "Eighteen Years Later - October 12th, 2024"
An alarm clock: 8:47 AM. Before it can ring, a hand shoots
out and silences it.
SOFIA RODRIGUEZ (18) sits up in bed. Latina, with her
mother's long dark hair and strong features. Beautiful in
that way girls are when they don't realize they're
beautiful. Tired eyes that have seen too much
responsibility. She's wearing an oversized t-shirt with a
faded logo.
She looks around her room: Walls covered with family
photos, a desk piled with textbooks and college brochures
(hidden under other papers), a bulletin board with a
calendar marked with everyone's schedules but her own.
Sofia picks up her phone. 47 missed calls and texts. She
scrolls through them without reading, already knowing what
they'll say.
She spots something on her desk: A COMMUNITY COLLEGE
BROCHURE. She grabs it quickly, shoves it under her
mattress. Can't let anyone see. Can't let anyone know she
wants something for herself.
From downstairs: The sound of voices. Her family. Already
needing something.
Sofia closes her eyes. Takes a breath. Becomes The Glue.
                    SOFIA
              (to herself, practiced)

                    It's your birthday. Just get
                    through today.
She gets up, pulls on jeans and a simple blouse. In the
mirror, she pauses. For just a moment, she sees herself.
Really sees herself. Eighteen years old and exhausted.
Her phone buzzes. Text from ABUELA: "Buenos días, mi
estrella. Watch the sky today."
Sofia frowns at the message. Weird. But then again, Abuela
is always weird.

                                                    CUT TO:

INT. RODRIGUEZ HOUSE - KITCHEN - CONTINUOUS
The kitchen is lived-in, warm, cluttered with life. A
calendar on the wall, marked in different colors for
different people. Sofia's entries are all in green.
Everyone else's are in their own colors.
RAMON RODRIGUEZ (45) stands at the counter, working on his
truck engine. He's got grease on his hands, under his
nails, on his work shirt. A machinist's build - strong but
tired. His face is weathered, handsome in a way that says
he used to smile more.
He's drinking coffee that's gone cold, staring at the
engine part like it's a puzzle he can't solve. Or maybe
like it's easier than looking at anything else.
Sofia enters. Ramon looks up, tries to smile.
                         RAMON
          Buenos días, mija. Happy birthday.
He says it like he's reading from a script. Not unkind.
Just... distant.
                         SOFIA
             (automatic smile, the one she always wears)
          Thanks, Dad.
She moves to the coffee pot, pours herself a cup. Black. No
sugar. No cream. The way people drink coffee when they need
it to work, not taste good.
                         RAMON
          Abuela's already up. She's in the
          backyard, talking to the plants
          again.
                         SOFIA
          She say what she wants for dinner?
                         RAMON
             (going back to his engine)
          I don't know. You'll have to ask
          her. I'm working the grill later.
Of course he is. Sofia nods. Adds "figure out dinner" to
the mental list that never ends.
Through the window: ABUELA RODRIGUEZ (72) in the backyard,
tending to her garden. She's wearing a flower-print dress
and sensible shoes. Her silver hair is pulled back. She
moves slow but deliberate, talking to the tomato plants in
Spanish.
Sofia watches her grandmother for a moment. Abuela stops,
looks up at the sky. Concerned. Then she looks directly at

the kitchen window - directly at Sofia - as if she knew
Sofia was watching all along.
Their eyes meet.
Abuela mouths something. Sofia can't quite make it out. But
it looked like: "The lightning knows."
Sofia shivers. Turns away.

                    RAMON
          You okay, mija?
                    SOFIA
          Yeah. Just... didn't sleep well.
                    RAMON
               (still not looking at her)
          You make a list for the party? I
          can pick up stuff after work.
                    SOFIA
               (pulling out her phone, showing
               him a detailed list)
Already sent it to you. Propane tanks are in the shed.
Chairs are in the garage.
                    RAMON
               (nodding, impressed but not surprised)
          You're good at this. What would we
          do without you?
Sofia doesn't answer. That's the question, isn't it?
The front door SLAMS open.
ANITA (16), Sofia's younger cousin, storms in. Defensive,
rebellious, wearing too much makeup and not enough
confidence. Her phone is surgically attached to her hand.
                    ANITA
               (to no one in particular)
          I don't want to be here.
                    RAMON
          Good morning to you too, Anita.
                    ANITA
               (ignoring him, to Sofia)
          Danny's coming today, and you
          can't say anything about it.
Sofia's jaw tightens. Danny. The boy with the gang
affiliations. The boy Anita thinks she loves.
                    SOFIA
          Anita, we talked about this--
                    ANITA
          No. YOU talked. I didn't agree to
          anything. It's Sofia's birthday,
          everyone's going to be here, and
          Danny's my boyfriend, so he's
          coming.
                    RAMON
               (still not looking up from his engine,
               useless)
          Girls...
                    SOFIA
               (carefully, diplomatically - The Glue at
               work)

                    I'm not saying he can't come. I'm
                    just saying... be careful. You
                    know what people say about him.
                              ANITA
                    People say a lot of things.
                    Doesn't make them true. Just
                    because you're scared of
                    everything doesn't mean I have to
                    be.
That lands. Sofia flinches.
                              ANITA
                        (softer, guilty)
                    I didn't mean--
                              SOFIA
                    It's fine. Bring Danny. Whatever.
                    I just want today to go smoothly.
                              ANITA
                        (defensive again, because apologizing is
                        hard)
                    Well maybe it will if everyone
                    stops trying to control
                    everything.
She storms upstairs. Sofia and Ramon are left in the
kitchen. Ramon finally looks up.
                              RAMON
                    She's just being sixteen.
                              SOFIA
                    I know.
                              RAMON
                    Her mom would know what to say.
Sofia goes very still. "Her mom" - Ramon's sister, who died
three years ago. Another person Sofia couldn't save.
                              SOFIA
                        (quiet)
                    Yeah. She would.
Silence. Ramon returns to his engine. Sofia drinks her
coffee.
A car horn HONKS outside. Three times. Happy and obnoxious.
Sofia's face lights up - genuine, not practiced. She
actually smiles.
                              SOFIA
                    That's Mateo.
                              RAMON
                    That boy's always early.
                              SOFIA
                        (heading to the door)
                    That boy's always on time. There's
                    a difference.
She's out the door before Ramon can respond. He watches her
go, something like sadness crossing his face. Then he goes
back to his engine.
                                                       CUT TO:

EXT. RODRIGUEZ HOUSE - CONTINUOUS

MATEO RODRIGUEZ (18) leans against a slightly beat-up Honda
Civic, grinning. He's wearing a clean white t-shirt and
jeans, his dark hair styled but not trying too hard. He's
got one of those faces that makes you trust him
immediately.
Sofia comes out, and for a second - just a second - she
lets herself be eighteen and happy instead of eighteen and
responsible.

                    MATEO
          Happy birthday, Sof.
He hands her a small wrapped box. Not expensive, but
thoughtful. She knows what it is before she opens it - a
keychain, with a little star charm. "Because you're a
star," he'd say, if he was the type to say things like that
out loud.

                    SOFIA
          You didn't have to--
                    MATEO
          I know. I wanted to.
They stand there, in that moment where something could
happen, or not happen. Sofia breaks it first. She always
does.

                    SOFIA
          So. Party's at two. You coming?
                    MATEO
               (playful)
          Would I miss Sofia Rodriguez's
          birthday party? The event of the
          season?
                    SOFIA
               (smiling, but tired)
          It's going to be a disaster.
                    MATEO
          Why? Everyone loves your parties.
                    SOFIA
          Everyone loves the parties I plan
          for them. Not the same thing.
Mateo notices something in her voice. Concern flickers
across his face.

                    MATEO
          You okay?
                    SOFIA
               (automatic response)
          I'm fine.
She's not fine. They both know it. But Mateo, being Mateo,
doesn't push.

                    MATEO
          Well, I'll be there at two. With
          food. Good food, not that
          supermarket cake your dad always
          gets.
That gets a real smile from her.
                    SOFIA
          Thanks, Mateo.

                         MATEO
                 (heading back to his car)
            Anything for you, Sof.
He means it. She knows he means it. And that makes it
harder, somehow.
Sofia watches him drive away, then looks down at the small
gift in her hand. The star keychain catches the morning
light.
Her phone buzzes. More texts. More needs.
She shoves the gift in her pocket and heads back inside.
                                                   CUT TO:

INT. COMMUNITY COLLEGE - ADMISSIONS OFFICE - 11:00 AM
Sofia sits across from COUNSELOR MARTINEZ (50s, kind face,
seen too many dreams deferred). The counselor's office is
small but warm. Posters on the wall: "Your Future Starts
Here" and "Education Opens Doors."
On the desk between them: An application. Incomplete.
                    COUNSELOR MARTINEZ
            Sofia, you have excellent grades.
            SAT scores that would get you into
            a four-year university. But you're
            applying here, to community
            college, for part-time enrollment.
                         SOFIA
            I need to stay local. Help with
            family.
                    COUNSELOR MARTINEZ
                 (gentle, but direct)
            And the part-time?
                         SOFIA
            I need to work. My family... they
            depend on me.
Counselor Martinez has heard this story before. Too many
times.
                    COUNSELOR MARTINEZ
            Sofia. What do you want?
The question catches Sofia off guard.
                         SOFIA
            What?
                    COUNSELOR MARTINEZ
            Not what your family needs. Not
            what's practical. What do YOU
            want? If you could do anything.
Sofia opens her mouth. Closes it. She doesn't have an
answer. She's never let herself think about it.
                         SOFIA
                 (quiet)
            It doesn't matter what I want.
                    COUNSELOR MARTINEZ
            It should. You're eighteen. You
            have your whole life ahead of you.
                         SOFIA
                 (a bitter laugh)
            Do I?

Her phone buzzes. Text from ANITA: "Where are you? Need you home. NOW."

Sofia stands.

                    SOFIA
          I have to go. Family emergency.

It's always a family emergency.

                    COUNSELOR MARTINEZ
          Sofia. The application deadline is
          next week. After that--

                    SOFIA
          I'll finish it. I promise.

Another promise she might not be able to keep.

                                        CUT TO:

EXT. RODRIGUEZ HOUSE - BACKYARD - 12:00 PM

The party is being set up. UNCLE JORGE (48, Ramon's brother, louder and more alive) arranges chairs. TIA SOFIA (50s, Jorge's wife, warm and gossipy) sets up a food table.

Sofia arrives, immediately slipping back into Organizer Mode.

                    SOFIA
          Tia Sofia, the tablecloths are in
          the garage. Jorge, those chairs
          need to be in rows of five, not
          four.

Everyone adjusts without question. This is what Sofia does. This is who she is.

Abuela stands near her garden, watching. Not helping. Just... watching.

Sofia notices her grandmother staring at the sky again.

                    SOFIA
               (approaching)
          Abuela? You okay?

                    ABUELA
               (not looking away from the sky)
          You were born under strange skies,
          mija. Lightning that came from
          nowhere.

                    SOFIA
          Mom told you about that?

                    ABUELA
          Your mother didn't need to tell
          me. I felt it. The moment you were
          born, the world... shifted.

Sofia doesn't know what to say to that. Abuela has always been a little strange, a little mystical.

                    SOFIA
          It's just my birthday, Abuela. No
          big deal.

                    ABUELA
               (finally looking at Sofia)
          Today is not just a birthday.
          Today, the lightning returns.

A chill runs down Sofia's spine. But before she can ask what Abuela means--

                              ANITA
                      (from the back gate)
                   Sofia! Danny's here!
Sofia turns. DANNY (17, trying too hard to look tough,
failing) walks in with Anita. He's wearing colors that make
Sofia's chest tighten - gang colors, subtle but there.
More concerning: There's a bulge in his jacket pocket.
Shape's all wrong. Sofia's seen enough to know what a gun
looks like, even hidden.
Ramon, at the grill, notices Danny. His jaw tightens.
OFFICER GARCIA (40s, family friend, off-duty cop in
civilian clothes) arrives with his wife. He notices Danny
too. The gun. His hand instinctively moves to his hip -
where his service weapon would be, if he was on duty.
Tension. Building.
Danny approaches Sofia, trying to be friendly.
                              DANNY
                   Hey, uh, Sofia. Happy birthday.
                              SOFIA
                      (watching his pocket)
                   Thanks, Danny.
                              ANITA
                      (oblivious)
                   Can Danny help set up? He's really
                   good with his hands.
The words hang there, innocent but also not. Sofia and
Danny both know what's in his pocket.
                              SOFIA
                   Sure. Danny, why don't you help
                   Uncle Jorge with the chairs?
She's trying to keep him away from the grill. Away from the
propane. Away from anything that could turn bad.
Danny nods, relieved. He heads toward the garage where
Jorge is setting up chairs.
As he walks away, Sofia notices: THREE GUYS standing across
the street. Watching. Waiting. They're not trying to hide.
They're sending a message.
Danny sees them too. His face goes pale.
                              ANITA
                      (following Sofia's gaze)
                   Who are they?
                              SOFIA
                      (lying)
                   I don't know. Probably nobody.
But they're not nobody. And Sofia knows it.
Abuela touches Sofia's shoulder.
                              ABUELA
                      (whispered)
                   The sky, mija. Don't forget to
                   watch the sky.
Sofia looks up. The sky is still clear. Still blue. Still
normal.
But there's something in the air. A charge. Like the moment
before a storm.

Sofia checks her phone: 12:15 PM.
Nineteen minutes.

                                                          CUT TO:

INT. RODRIGUEZ HOUSE - LIVING ROOM - 12:25 PM
The party is starting. People arrive: neighbors, distant
relatives, coworkers of Ramon's. The house fills with
voices, laughter, life.
Sofia moves through it all, smiling, thanking people for
coming, making sure everyone has food and drinks. Always
moving. Never still.
Mateo arrives, right on time, and finds her in the kitchen.

                    MATEO
          You okay? You seem... tense.
                    SOFIA
          I'm fine. Just want everything to
          go well.
                    MATEO
          It will. It always does.
                    SOFIA
              (something in her voice)
          Does it?

Before he can answer, Danny rushes past them, looking
panicked. The three guys from across the street are now at
the fence, calling to him.

                    GANG MEMBER #1
          Danny! We need to talk!

Ramon, standing at the grill with tongs, notices.

                    RAMON
          Who the hell is that?

Officer Garcia, who stayed for the party, tenses. His cop
instincts kicking in.

                    OFFICER GARCIA
          That's Tony Martinez and his crew.
          They're...

He doesn't finish. He doesn't need to.
Anita, defensive, steps toward the fence.

                    ANITA
          They're Danny's friends!
                    SOFIA
              (grabbing Anita's arm)
          Anita, stay inside.
                    ANITA
              (pulling away)
          Don't tell me what to do!

Everything is happening too fast. The party, which was
calm, is now electric with tension.
Danny, scared, reaches into his pocket.
Sofia sees it.

                    SOFIA
          Danny, don't!

But the gang members see the movement. They start forward.
Officer Garcia moves to intervene. Ramon drops his tongs,
starting toward the fence.
Chaos. Everyone moving at once.

And then--
A sound. Not thunder. Something else.
Everyone stops. Looks up.
The sky, which was clear, is suddenly dark. Storm clouds
from nowhere, rolling in impossibly fast.

                    ABUELA
              (from the porch, calm)
         It's time.
Sofia checks her phone: 12:33 PM.
One minute.
The wind picks up. Leaves swirling. The temperature drops
ten degrees in seconds.
Everyone in the backyard is confused, looking at the sky,
at each other, trying to understand what's happening.
Danny, panicked, pulls the gun fully out of his pocket.

                    DANNY
         Stay back!
No one was advancing. But fear makes people do stupid
things.
The gang members see the gun. They scatter. Running.
Officer Garcia reaches for his own weapon, then remembers
he's off duty. Unarmed.

                    OFFICER GARCIA
         Danny, put the gun down!
Ramon is still moving forward, not thinking, just reacting.

                    RAMON
         Get away from my family!
Jorge tries to stop his brother.

                    JORGE
         Ramon, wait--
Too many people moving. Too much chaos.
Danny, terrified, backpedals. Stumbles. The gun tumbles
from his hand, hits the ground near the grill, near the
propane tanks.
Sofia sees it all happening in slow motion.
The gun. The propane. The chaos.
And in the sky: BALL LIGHTNING.
It forms from nothing. A sphere of crackling energy, purple
and blue and white, hovering above the party like a
malevolent star.
Everyone sees it. Everyone stops.

                    OFFICER GARCIA
              (whispered)
         What the hell is that?
The ball lightning descends. Slowly. Deliberately. Like
it's looking for something.
Abuela, on the porch, is calm. She's seen this before.

                    ABUELA
              (to Sofia, across the yard)
         It's looking for you, mija.
Sofia stands frozen. Mateo grabs her hand.

                    MATEO
         What is that thing?
                    SOFIA

                    I don't... I don't know.
But she does know. Somewhere deep inside, she knows.
The ball lightning moves closer. It's at fence height now.
People back away, terrified.
And then--
The gun. Someone - Ramon, maybe, or Jorge, or Danny trying
to grab it back - kicks it. Accidentally. It discharges.
BANG.
The bullet hits a propane tank.
For one perfect second: Nothing.
Everyone stares at the propane tank. At the bullet hole.
Then--
WHOOOOSH.
The propane ignites.
Fire everywhere. The explosion is small at first, then
catches the second tank.
People scream. Running. Chaos.
Sofia tries to move, but there's fire between her and the
house, between her and everyone she loves.
The ball lightning, still hovering, pulses.
Ramon is on the ground, thrown by the blast.
Anita is screaming.
Mateo is pulling Sofia away from the fire.
And through it all: The ball lightning descends. Directly
toward Sofia.
She looks up at it. It's beautiful and terrible and
impossible.
                    SOFIA
            (to the lightning, to the
            universe, to whatever's listening)
What do you want from me?!
The lightning reaches her.
Touch.
Pure white light. Everything washed away.
For a moment, Sofia sees: Her mother's face. Maria,
smiling, saying something Sofia can't hear. Then darkness.
Then--
NOTHING.
BLACK.
Sound of an alarm clock.
Beep. Beep. Beep.
                    SMASH CUT TO
INT. SOFIA'S BEDROOM - MORNING
The alarm: 8:47 AM.
Sofia sits bolt upright in bed. Gasping. Trembling.
She looks around wildly. Her room. Her bed. Her things.
She grabs her phone. Checks the date.
October 12th.
Her birthday.
                    SOFIA
            (whispered, terrified)
        No. No no no no no.
She jumps out of bed, runs to the window. Outside: The day
is just starting. The morning sun. Everything normal.

From downstairs: Her father's voice. Working on his engine.
RAMON (O.S.)
Sofia! You up?
Sofia's hands are shaking. She checks her body. No burns.
No injuries.
The party hasn't happened yet.
Or it happened and... and...
Her phone buzzes. Text from Abuela: "Buenos días, mi
estrella. Watch the sky today."
The same text. The exact same text.
Sofia backs away from the phone like it's going to bite
her.
Another buzz. Mateo: "Happy birthday! Can't wait to see
you. Party's at two, right?"
It's starting over. All of it.
                    SOFIA
            (to herself, breaking)
        This isn't real. This isn't
        happening.
But it is happening.
She sits on her bed. Puts her head in her hands.
The day is starting over. And she's the only one who knows.
She's trapped.
And she has no idea how to get out.
                                        FADE TO:

INT. SOFIA'S BEDROOM - MORNING (8:47 AM)

Sofia's eyes snap open. She stares at the ceiling.

                    SOFIA
        No. No no no no.

She grabs her phone. 8:47 AM. Birthday notifications.

Her door opens. Abuela stands there, smiling.

                    ABUELA
        Buenos días, mi estrella! Feliz
cumpleaños!

Sofia's face goes white.

                    SOFIA
            (whispered)
        It's happening again.

INT. SOFIA'S KITCHEN - CONTINUOUS

Sofia stumbles to the kitchen. Everything is exactly the
same.

Ramon at the table with grease on his hands. The same
newspaper.
The same coffee mug in the exact same spot.

                    RAMON
          Happy birthday, mija.

                    SOFIA
          Dad, I... I think something's
wrong.

He looks up.

                    RAMON
          You okay?

                    SOFIA
          I don't know. I think... Did we
already do this?

                    RAMON
          Do what?

She looks around. The clock says 8:52 AM. Five minutes.
Just
like last time.

                    SOFIA
          Nothing. I'm fine.

But she's not fine.

EXT. SOFIA'S BACKYARD - DAY (11:30 AM)

The party is setting up. Exactly the same.

Sofia watches everything with growing horror. Uncle Jorge
arrives. Same greeting. Same awkwardness. She smooths it
over
again, automatically.

Mateo arrives with flowers. Same flowers.

                    MATEO
          Happy birthday! These are for—

                    SOFIA
          Daisies. You brought daisies.

                    MATEO
          Yeah... you okay?

She's shaking.

                    SOFIA
          Do you remember anything weird
happening? Like... earlier?

                    MATEO
          Earlier? It's barely noon.

                    SOFIA
          Right. Yeah. Sorry.

She tries to warn people. They don't listen. Nobody
believes
her.

The clouds come. 12:15 PM. Right on schedule.

The gang arrives. 12:20 PM.

Danny gets nervous. Pulls the gun.

Sofia screams this time: "NO! Don't!"

But chaos erupts anyway. The gun falls.

BOOM.

The propane explodes.

Everything goes white.

And this time, as she dies, Sofia SEES it clearly - a
sphere
of crackling blue-white energy forming in the air above
her.

Ball lightning.

It's looking directly at her.

DARKNESS.

INT. SOFIA'S BEDROOM - MORNING (8:47 AM)

Sofia gasps awake, tears streaming down her face.

                    SOFIA
          Oh God. Oh God oh God oh God.

She's really trapped.

                    SMASH CUT TO
INT. SOFIA'S KITCHEN - MORNING (9:15 AM)

Sofia is on the phone, pacing.

                    SOFIA
          Officer Garcia? It's Sofia
          RODRIGUEZ.
I need you to come to my party
today... Yes, I know it's my
birthday... No, there's going to
be trouble... Please, just trust
me.

She hangs up. Takes a breath.

Abuela watches from the doorway.

                    ABUELA
          What kind of trouble, mija?

EXT. SOFIA'S BACKYARD - DAY (12:00 PM)

The party is going. Officer Garcia is there in uniform,
standing near the fence.

Sofia keeps looking at the street. Waiting.

12:20 PM comes and goes. No gang.

                    SOFIA
                 (to herself)
          They're not coming. They're not
coming.

She starts to relax. Maybe she fixed it.

12:25 PM.

Anita and Danny are by the propane tanks, arguing. Sofia
wasn't watching them.

                    ANITA
          Just show me!

Danny nervously pulls out the gun to prove he has it. To
show
her he's tough.

A bottle falls off a table behind them. Loud crash.

Danny jumps. The gun slips.

It hits the concrete.

BANG.

The propane tanks—

BOOM.

DARKNESS.

EXT. SOFIA'S BACKYARD - DAY (12:34 PM)

Sofia is dying. Blood. Pain. Ringing in her ears.

The clouds part.

Ball lightning forms - a perfect sphere of crackling energy,
beautiful and terrible.

It descends slowly.

Sofia tries to crawl away but can't move. The lightning
reaches her.

                    SOFIA
               (whispered)
          Please...

It touches her.

Everything goes white.

                    SMASH CUT TO
INT. SOFIA'S BEDROOM - MORNING (8:47 AM)

Sofia wakes up screaming.

                    SOFIA
          The lightning! The lightning comes
for me!

Abuela rushes in.

                    ABUELA
          Mija! You're okay! Just a dream—

                    SOFIA
          It's not a dream! It's real! I
          keep
dying! And the lightning... it
always comes at 12:34!

Abuela stares at her. Something shifts in her eyes.

                         ABUELA
          12:34?

                         SOFIA
          Yes! Exactly 12:34! Why?

                         ABUELA
          That's when you were born. To the
minute.

MONTAGE -

-- Sofia calls and cancels the party. Uncle Jorge shows up
anyway. The explosion still happens. She dies at 12:34.

-- Sofia physically blocks Danny from entering. Anita
rebels,
sneaks him in through the side gate. Explosion. 12:34.

-- Sofia removes all the propane tanks early in the
morning.
Ramon brings more for the grill. Explosion. 12:34.

-- Sofia survives one explosion, makes it to 12:34. Ball
lightning appears in clear sky. Strikes her directly.
Reset.

                       SMASH CUT TO
INT. ABUELA'S ROOM - MORNING (10:00 AM)

Sofia sits on the edge of Abuela's bed. She's exhausted.
Dark
circles under her eyes.

                         SOFIA
          Tell me about the day I was born.
Everything.

Abuela sits in her chair, hands folded.

                         ABUELA
          Your mother... she was in labor
          for
eighteen hours. You were breech.
The doctors were worried.

                         SOFIA
          And the lightning?

                         ABUELA
          It was a clear day. Sunny. Then

suddenly, dark clouds. Just over
the hospital. The doctors said
they'd never seen anything like
it.

She pauses. Remembering.

                    ABUELA (CONT'D)
          At 12:34 exactly, as you were
being born, ball lightning came
through the window. Rolled across
the ceiling. The doctors were
shouting, trying to shield your
mother. And then...

                    SOFIA
          What?

                    ABUELA
          It hovered over you. Just for a
moment. A ball of light, beautiful
and terrible. Then it vanished.

                    SOFIA
          Did it hurt anyone?

                    ABUELA
          No. That's what was strange. It
didn't hurt anyone. The doctors
called it a miracle. Said you were
born in a moment between moments.

Sofia absorbs this.

                    SOFIA
          What does that mean?

                    ABUELA
          I don't know, mija. But your
          mother
always said you were especial.
Marked for something important.

                    SOFIA
          Important enough to die over and
over?

Abuela reaches out, takes Sofia's hand.

                    ABUELA
          You were born touched by
          lightning.
Maybe... maybe it's trying to tell
you something.

EXT. SOFIA'S BACKYARD - DAY (11:45 AM)

Sofia watches Danny arrive. She's been waiting.

She pulls him aside immediately.

                    SOFIA
          You have a gun.

Danny's eyes go wide.

                    DANNY
          How did you—

                    SOFIA
          Give it to me. Right now.

                    DANNY
          I can't. I need it for—

                    SOFIA
          For what? Protection? From who?

Danny looks around nervously.

                    DANNY
          There are guys. They think I owe
them. They might come here.

                    SOFIA
          They won't. And even if they do,
that gun will kill everyone.
Please. Trust me.

Something in her voice. Danny hesitates, then reaches into
his waistband.

He hands her the gun.

Officer Garcia is nearby. Sofia immediately walks over,
hands
it to him.

                    SOFIA
          Keep this safe until after the
party.

Garcia looks surprised but takes it.

                    GARCIA
          You okay, Sofia?

                         SOFIA
                I will be. Maybe.

EXT. SOFIA'S BACKYARD - DAY (12:25 PM)

The party is going smoothly. No gun. No gang showed up. No
explosion.

Sofia watches the clock on her phone. 12:26... 12:27...

She's sweating. Her heart is pounding.

Mateo sits next to her.

                         MATEO
                You've been weird all day. What's
going on?

                         SOFIA
                In seven minutes, something is
going to happen.

                         MATEO
                What?

                         SOFIA
                I don't know how to explain it.

12:32.

The sky is still clear.

12:33.

Sofia stands up. Everyone is eating, talking, laughing.
Normal. Safe.

12:34.

The clouds come.

Not gradually. Instantly. Like a curtain being pulled.

The temperature drops.

                         RAMON
                What the hell?

Everyone looks up.

Ball lightning forms in the sky. A perfect sphere of
crackling
energy, about three feet wide. Blue-white. Pulsing.

It descends slowly toward the party.

People start screaming.

Sofia stands there, frozen. Watching it come.

                    MATEO
          Sofia! RUN!

But she doesn't run. She's transfixed.

The ball lightning reaches her. Hovers three feet in front
of
her face.

She can feel the energy. Her hair standing on end. Ozone
smell.

                    SOFIA
               (whispered)
          What do you want?

It pulses. Bright. Then brighter.

It strikes.

Everything goes white.

DARKNESS.

                    SMASH CUT TO
INT. SOFIA'S BEDROOM - MORNING (8:47 AM)

Sofia wakes up. Stares at the ceiling.

                    SOFIA
          It's not trying to kill me. It's
looking FOR me.

INT. ABUELA'S ROOM - MORNING (10:30 AM)

Sofia is determined now. Less scared. More focused.

                    SOFIA
          Tell me about when I was nine. The
storm.

Abuela's face changes. Old fear.

                    ABUELA
          How do you know about that?

                         SOFIA
              I just do. Please.

Abuela nods slowly.

                         ABUELA
              It was summer. A freak storm. Ball
lightning appeared in our backyard.

She closes her eyes, remembering.

              FLASHBACK - NINE YEARS AGO

EXT. BACKYARD - DAY

9-year-old SOFIA stands in the yard. Ball lightning hovers
near the fence. Beautiful. Hypnotic.

Young Sofia starts walking toward it. Slowly. Like she's
being
called.

ABUELA (O.S.)
                         SOFIA! NO!

Abuela runs out, grabs young Sofia, pulls her back inside.

Young Sofia is crying.

                         YOUNG SOFIA
              It was pretty...

                         ABUELA
              Never go toward the lightning. You
hear me? Never!

                         YOUNG SOFIA
              Why?

                         ABUELA
              Because it wants something from
you. And I don't know what.

              BACK TO PRESENT

INT. ABUELA'S ROOM - CONTINUOUS

Abuela opens her eyes.

                         ABUELA
              I was so scared. I thought it
              would

take you from me.

                    SOFIA
          But it didn't. It left.

                    ABUELA
          Yes. After a few minutes, it
          just...
vanished.

Sofia thinks about this.

                    SOFIA
          Maybe... maybe you pulling me back
is what made it leave.

                    ABUELA
          What do you mean?

                    SOFIA
          What if I was supposed to go
toward it? And you stopped me?

Abuela looks stricken.

                    ABUELA
          No. I saved you.

                    SOFIA
          Did you? Or did you just delay
this?

Long pause.

                    ABUELA
          What are you saying?

                    SOFIA
          I'm saying maybe the lightning has
been waiting. For today. For my
18th birthday. And maybe I need
to stop running from it.

MONTAGE:

-- Sofia investigates Uncle Jorge. Watches him closely.
Nothing suspicious.

-- She asks Ramon about Mom's death. He breaks down. "She
was
driving to help Jorge. It was just an accident. A car
accident. Nothing more."

-- Jorge confesses his guilt. "If I hadn't called... she'd

still be alive. But it wasn't gangs. Wasn't violence.
Just...
bad timing."

-- Sofia realizes: Uncle isn't the danger. He never was.

-- She removes the gun early. Party goes smoothly. 12:34 -
ball lightning comes anyway. She runs. It strikes her
anyway.
Reset.

-- She hides inside at 12:30. Locks everyone in. 12:34 -
ball
lightning appears INSIDE THE HOUSE. Passes through walls.
Finds her. Strikes. Reset.

                    SMASH CUT TO
INT. SOFIA'S BEDROOM - MORNING (8:47 AM)

Sofia wakes up. She sits up slowly.

                    SOFIA
          You can't be escaped. You can't be
hidden from. You're not trying to
kill me.

She gets out of bed.

                    SOFIA (CONT'D)
          You're trying to give me
          something.

                    SMASH CUT TO
EXT. SOFIA'S BACKYARD - DAY (12:34 PM)

Sofia has removed the gun, removed the propane. The
party is safe.

She stands in the center of the yard. Waiting.

Everyone else is inside. She made them go in. Mateo watches
from the window, worried.

12:34.

The clouds come.

Ball lightning forms. Descends.

Sofia doesn't run. Doesn't hide. Stands there.

The ball lightning approaches. Hovers two feet in front of
her.

She reaches out her hand.

                         SOFIA
              I'm not afraid of you.

The lightning pulses. Bright.

She touches it.

FLASH.

                   VISION - FRAGMENTED IMAGES

-- Her mother's face in the hospital. Smiling. Exhausted.
Happy.

-- Ball lightning hovering over newborn Sofia.

-- Her mother's voice: "Protect her. Let her LIVE."

-- A choice being made. A sacrifice.

-- The word "LIVE" written in electricity.

                        BACK TO REALITY

Sofia gasps. Pulls her hand back.

She looks around.

Everyone is FROZEN.

Mid-motion. Mid-sentence. Completely still.

Time has stopped.

Only Sofia can move.

She walks through the frozen party. Touches Mateo's frozen
hand.

                         SOFIA
              What is this?

She looks at the ball lightning. It's still there.
Hovering.
Watching.

                      SOFIA (CONT'D)
              Did you do this?

The clock on someone's frozen phone: 12:34. Not moving.

Sofia walks back to the center. Faces the lightning.

                         SOFIA (CONT'D)
              What do you want from me?

The lightning pulses once. Bright.

Then the clock ticks: 12:35.

Everything unfreezes.

People gasp, confused, looking around.
                         RAMON
              Did you... did you all see that
light?
                         JORGE
              What was that?
But Sofia is still standing there. Alive. The lightning is
gone.

Mateo runs out to her.

                         MATEO
              Sofia! Are you okay?

She nods slowly.

                         SOFIA
              I'm alive. I'm still alive.

The party continues, people shaken but okay. Evening comes.

Sofia goes to bed.

And wakes up at 8:47 AM.

She sits up in bed, not panicking this time. Thinking.
                         SOFIA
              Surviving isn't enough. There's
something I need to do. Something
I need to become.

                         SMASH CUT TO
INT. PROTAGONIST'S BEDROOM - MORNING

SOFIA RODRIGUEZ (18) wakes up. Again. The same cumbia music
from downstairs. The same smell of pan dulce and coffee.
She doesn't even flinch anymore.
SOFIA (V.O.)
I've tried being nice. I've tried being smart. I've
gathered all the information. Time to try something stupid.
She sits up, looks at her hands. Steady. Or maybe just
numb.

INT. ABUELA'S BEDROOM - MOMENTS LATER
Sofia moves quietly, efficiently. She's done this before--
the creeping, the careful stepping over the squeaky
floorboard. But this time she's not just snooping.
She kneels beside Abuela's bed, reaches under. The shoebox
is there, behind the other shoeboxes that actually have
shoes. She pulls it out.
Opens it.
The gun sits there. Old. A revolver. Smith & Wesson .38
Special. She's learned this already when she looked but
didn't touch.
SOFIA (V.O.)
My abuela keeps a gun under her bed. This fact has occupied
approximately forty-seven percent of my brain space for the
last ten times. The other fifty-three percent keeps
replaying the explosion.
She picks it up. Heavier than she expected. Colder.
SOFIA (V.O.)
I don't know whose gun this was. Maybe Abuelo's before he
died. Maybe Jorge's before he went to prison. Maybe it
doesn't matter. Maybe all that matters is stopping them
from coming.
INT. SOFIA'S BEDROOM - CONTINUOUS
Sofia sits on her bed. Gun on her lap. She pulls out her
phone, searches "how to load a revolver."
SOFIA (V.O.)
YouTube is very helpful when you're planning to do
something incredibly fucking stupid. Sorry, Mom. I know
you're watching from heaven or whatever. Sorry you have to
see this version of your daughter.
She practices the motion. Opening the cylinder. Checking.
Closing it. The click is loud in the quiet room.
ABUELA (O.S.)
                    (from downstairs)
          Mija! Ven a desayunar!
Sofia flinches. Hides the gun under her pillow.
SOFIA (V.O.)
I have seven hours until they show up. Seven hours to
decide if I'm really going to do this. Seven hours to
become someone I'm not.
                    TIME CUT - SERIES OF SHOTS
          - Sofia at breakfast, barely
          eating, watching her DAD talk
          about work
- Sofia helping set up decorations, the gun a weight in her
mind
- Sofia standing in front of the bathroom mirror, face pale
- The GUN, wrapped in a small towel, in her purse
INT. LIVING ROOM - EARLY EVENING
The party's in full swing. Family everywhere. Sofia's
younger cousins running around. Tías gossiping. The BANDA
music too loud. Her shy BOYFRIEND, DANNY, standing
awkwardly by the chips.
Then--

The front door opens.
JORGE walks in. Mid-forties. Lean. Tattoos creeping up his
neck. But his face is soft, nervous. He's carrying flowers.
The room goes quiet. Just like it always does.
ABUELA gasps. Covers her mouth.
DAD (RAMÓN)'s face goes dark. Sofia sees his jaw clench.
SOFIA (V.O.)
Here we go. Every time, I see my dad's face break. Every
instance, I see him try to decide between anger and love.
Every loop, he chooses anger. Can't blame him. His brother
didn't even call.

                    RAMÓN
          What the fuck, Jorge?
                    ABUELA
          Ramón--
                    RAMÓN
          No, Ma. What the FUCK? You're out?
          When? You call? You let us know?
          Nothing?
                    JORGE
               (quiet)
          I wanted to surprise--
                    RAMÓN
          You wanted to surprise? On my
          daughter's birthday? On Sofia's
          day? You make this about YOU?
Sofia watches this dance. She's seen it ten times. Knows
every beat.
But this time, she feels the weight of the gun in her purse
on the kitchen counter.
This time, she knows what's coming in three hours.
EXT. BACKYARD - TWO HOURS LATER
The party's moved outside. Someone set up lights. The banda
gave way to norteño, then back to banda. Sofia's sitting on
the back steps, watching.
DANNY sits next to her, doesn't say anything. That's his
way. Comfortable silence.
Sofia looks at her cousin ANITA (16) dancing with her
boyfriend, LUIS. He's laughing. Seems sweet. But Sofia
knows, she followed him. Saw him throw signs. Saw which
corners he stood on.
SOFIA (V.O.)
Luis isn't a bad guy. He's just a guy who grew up on bad
blocks. But his homies know Jorge is out. And his homies
have homies who have enemies. And now everyone knows where
we live.
                    DANNY
          You okay?
Sofia looks at him. Really looks at him. In all this time,
this is the first time she's really looked at her
boyfriend.
                    SOFIA
          Danny, I need to ask you
          something.

                         DANNY
              Okay.
                         SOFIA
              If you knew something bad was
              going to happen... something
              really bad... and the only way to
              stop it was to do something
              worse... would you?
                         DANNY
                    (thinking)
              I don't know. Depends on the bad
              thing.
                         SOFIA
              People dying.
Danny's eyes widen.
                         DANNY
              Sofia, what--
                         SOFIA
              Just answer.
                         DANNY
                    (slowly)
              Then... yeah. I guess. If people
              were really going to die. But--
                         SOFIA
              But what?
                         DANNY
              But are you sure doing something
              worse is the only way? Like...
              really sure?
Sofia stares at the ground. Is she?
SOFIA (V.O.)
Shit. He's right. I haven't tried everything. I've tried
talking, I've tried warning, I've tried preventing Tío from
coming. But I haven't tried...
She looks at the cop neighbor's house. Officer MENDEZ's
truck in the driveway.
SOFIA (V.O.)
...actual help.
EXT. FRONT YARD - ONE HOUR LATER (9:45 PM)
Sofia watches the street. Waiting.
She left her purse inside. Left the gun inside.
Instead, she's standing with her DAD and JORGE, talking.
Actually talking. She forced it--pulled them both outside,
told them they needed to deal with their shit or leave her
party.
It's working. Sort of. They're not hugging it out, but
they're talking.
Then--
Two cars roll up. Slow. Too slow.
Sofia's stomach drops. Here it comes.
The back window of the lead car slides down.
But this time--
JORGE sees them. Tenses.
                         SOFIA

                              (to her dad)
                    Get inside. Now.
                         RAMÓN
               What--
                         SOFIA
               NOW!
She's already running. Not to the house. To Officer
MENDEZ's door.
She pounds on it. POUNDS.
                         SOFIA
                    Officer Mendez! Please! There's--
The door opens. OFFICER MENDEZ (40s, kind face, tired eyes)
looks confused.
                    OFFICER MENDEZ
                    Sofia? What's--
                         SOFIA
                    There are gang members outside my
                    house! They're here to hurt my
                    uncle! Please, you have to--
A GUNSHOT rings out.
Then another.
Then several.
OFFICER MENDEZ is already moving, radio to his mouth,
shouting codes.
Sofia runs back toward her house.
Everything is chaos.
Her family is screaming, running inside.
Her JORGE is on the ground--shot in the shoulder.
The cars are already peeling away.
                         SOFIA
                         (screaming)
                    No no no no--
Officer Mendez is there, applying pressure to the wound,
shouting into his radio.
More shots--from the backyard.
Sofia's heart stops.
SOFIA (V.O.)
The explosion always comes from the back.
She runs around the side of the house--
Just in time to see LUIS, panicked, running from the
backyard gate.
                         SOFIA
                    Luis! What did you--
                         LUIS
                    They made me! I swear, I didn't
                    want--
She shoves past him.
The backyard--
A device. Crude. Sitting by the propane tank for the grill.
Sofia's hands shake. She doesn't know how to defuse a bomb.
She's eighteen. She's supposed to be worried about
financial aid deadlines.
She grabs it. Just grabs it. Runs toward the back fence--
BOOM.

                         SMASH CUT TO
                    Sofia wakes up screaming.
Her hands are fine. No burns. No blood.
She screams anyway.
SOFIA (V.O.)
I died. I actually fucking died this time. I felt it. The
heat, the pressure, the-- Jesus Christ I'm going to throw
up.
She runs to her bathroom. Vomits.
Sits on the tile floor, shaking.
SOFIA (V.O.)
Okay. Okay. So we learned some things. One: Calling the
cops doesn't stop it. Two: The bomb is Luis's job, but he
doesn't want to do it. Three: Even if we stop the shooting,
they have a backup plan. Four: I am not a fucking action
hero. Five: There has to be another way.
She stands. Looks at herself in the mirror. Eyes red. Hair
a mess.
SOFIA (V.O.)
I can't keep doing this alone. I need help. Real help. But
who's going to believe me?
INT. LIVING ROOM - MORNING
Sofia comes downstairs in her pajamas. Everyone's already
there--her dad drinking coffee, Abuela making breakfast,
her little cousins already running around even though it's
only 8 AM.
She sits at the table. Takes a deep breath.
                              SOFIA
                    I need to tell you all something.
Her dad looks up from his phone. Abuela pauses mid-stir.
                              RAMÓN
                    What's wrong, mija?
                              SOFIA
                    I've been living the same day over
                    and over. Today. My birthday. For
                    almost two weeks now.
Silence. Her younger cousin MATEO (12) looks up from his
cereal.
                              MATEO
                    Like Groundhog Day?
                              SOFIA
                    Exactly like Groundhog Day.
                              RAMÓN
                         (concerned)
                    Sofia, have you been sleeping
                    okay? Maybe we should--
                              SOFIA
                    Dad, I'm not having a breakdown.
                    Listen. Tonight, at my party,
                    Jorge is going to show up. Out of
                    prison. No warning. And when he
                    does, people are going to come

                    after him. Gang members. They're
                    going to try to kill him. And us.
Abuela drops her spoon. It clatters on the counter.
                         ABUELA
                    (whispered)
                    How do you know this?
                         SOFIA
                    Because I've watched it happen
                    thirteen times. I've tried to stop
                    it thirteen times. And I keep
                    failing.
She's crying now. Not dramatic. Just... exhausted.
                         SOFIA (CONT'D)
                    I don't expect you to believe me.
                    I wouldn't believe me either. But
                    I'm telling you anyway because I
                    can't do this alone anymore.
Her father stands. Crosses to her. Puts his hand on her
shoulder.
                         RAMÓN
                    Okay. Let's say I believe you.
                    What do we do?
Sofia looks up at him, surprised.
                         SOFIA
                    You... you believe me?
                         RAMÓN
                    I don't know. Maybe. But you're my
                    daughter, and you're scared, and
                    that's enough. So what do we do?
Sofia takes a shaky breath.
                         SOFIA
                    I don't know yet. But thank you.
                    Thank you for listening.
                         TIME CUT
EXT. CORNER STORE - AFTERNOON
Sofia sits on the curb outside a bodega. An OLD MAN, CHUY
(70s, weathered face, seen too much), sits next to her.
He's smoking. Doesn't offer her one.
                         CHUY
                    Your uncle was always trouble.
                         SOFIA
                    You knew him? From before?
                         CHUY
                    Everyone knew Marcos. Smart kid.
                    Too smart. Started running for the
                    Culebras when he was fourteen. By
                    sixteen, he was moving real
                    weight.
Sofia sits very still.
                         SOFIA
                    What happened?
                         CHUY

What always happens. Got busted.
Big deal. Federal case. They had
him dead to rights.
                    SOFIA
What did he do?
                    CHUY
He testified. He cut a deal. Got
three years instead of fifteen.
And he gave names.
Sofia's stomach drops.
SOFIA (V.O.)
Oh. Oh shit. That's why he showed up out of nowhere. He
can't go back to his neighborhood. He can't go to his old
places. We're all he has left. And by coming here, he
brought them to us.
                    SOFIA
So they're coming for him.
Tonight.
                    CHUY
They're always coming, mija. If
not tonight, tomorrow. If not
tomorrow, next week. Your uncle is
a dead man walking. And anyone
around him when they catch up...
He doesn't finish. Doesn't need to.
Sofia stands there, frozen.
SOFIA (V.O.)
I can't stop them from coming. I can't convince Tío not to
come. I can't get the cops to camp out at my house all
night. I can't use violence without becoming just like
them. So what CAN I do?
                    CHUY
               (standing)
My advice? Tell your uncle to
leave. Tonight, before the party.
Tell him to run. Maybe he gets a
head start. Maybe he survives a
little longer.
He walks away.
Sofia stands there as the sun starts to set.
SOFIA (V.O.)
Tell him to run. But if he runs, he's alone forever. No
family. No home. Just running until they catch him. That's
not saving him. That's just... delaying. But if he stays...
we all die.
She looks at her phone. 6:47 PM.
Three hours until the party really starts.
Four hours until Jorge shows up.
Just over four hours until the explosion.
SOFIA (V.O.)
There has to be a third option. There has to be something
I'm not seeing. Some way to protect him AND keep everyone
safe. But what? What am I missing?
She starts walking home.

SOFIA (V.O.)
Maybe... maybe the answer isn't about stopping them. Maybe
it's about changing HIM. Changing all of us. Maybe the loop
isn't about the explosion. Maybe it's about the fact that
we're all so busy keeping secrets and protecting each other
that we can't actually save each other.
She stops walking.
SOFIA (V.O.)
Holy shit. That's it. That's it. The problem isn't the
gang. The problem is that we're all lying. Tío lied about
getting out. Dad lied about knowing Tío's past. I've been
lying by trying to fix everything alone. We're all so busy
being the glue that we forgot glue only works when pieces
actually touch each other.
She starts running.
SOFIA (V.O.)
I need to tell them. All of them. The truth. All of it.
Before Tío shows up. Before the gang. Before any of it. I
need to break this thing open.
INT. RODRIGUEZ HOUSE - EARLY EVENING
Sofia bursts through the front door.
Her family is setting up for the party. Decorations. Food.
Laughter.
She stands in the doorway, breathing hard.
                SOFIA
        Everyone stop.
They all look at her.
                SOFIA
        I need to tell you something. And
        you're not going to like it. And
        you're not going to believe me.
        But I need you to listen anyway.
Her dad puts down the banner he was hanging.
                RAMÓN
        Mija, what--
                SOFIA
        Jorge is getting out of prison
        today. He's going to show up here.
        Tonight. At my party.
Shocked silence.
                SOFIA
        And when he shows up, people who
        want him dead are going to follow
        him here. Because he testified
        against them. He cut a deal. He's
        a snitch. And they don't forgive
        that.
                ABUELA
        Sofia, how do you--
                SOFIA
        I know because I've lived this day
        fourteen times. I've watched you
        all die fourteen times. I've tried
        to stop it alone fourteen times.

                         And I can't. I can't fix this
                         alone. I need help. I need YOU.
She's crying now. Again. But different this time. Not
desperate. Not scared. Just... honest.
                         SOFIA
                    I know you think I'm crazy. I know
                    this sounds impossible. But I'm
                    asking you to trust me anyway.
                    Just this once. Can we please,
                    PLEASE, for once in our lives,
                    just be honest with each other?
Her dad stands there, mouth open. Abuela has tears in her
eyes.
And then--
The doorbell rings.
They all turn to look.
SOFIA (V.O.)
He's early. He's never early. I changed something. By
telling them, I changed something. This is new. This is--
Sofia walks to the door.
Opens it.
JORGE stands there. Flowers in hand. Fear in his eyes.
But he's not alone.
Two police officers stand behind him.
                         OFFICER #1
                    Are you Sofia RODRIGUEZ?
                         SOFIA
                         (confused)
                    Yes?
                         OFFICER #1
                    Your uncle here called us on his
                    way over. Said he had information
                    about a potential threat to this
                    residence. Said his niece warned
                    him somehow. Mind if we come in?
Sofia stares at Jorge.
He looks at her. Really looks at her.
                         JORGE
                         (quiet)
                    I don't know how you knew. But...
                    thank you. For trying.
SOFIA (V.O.)
I told the truth. And somehow, across the loops, across the
resets, across everything... he heard it. Someone finally
heard it.
She steps aside.
                         SOFIA
                    Please. Come in.
                                                      FADE TO:

THE PARTY - LATER
There are cops stationed outside. Plain clothes. Watching.
The party happens anyway. Smaller. More tense. But
happening.
Sofia watches the clock. 10:30 PM. Almost time.

Danny sits next to her.
                    DANNY
          Are you okay?
                    SOFIA
          I don't know yet.
10:45 PM.
A car rolls by. Slow. Too slow.
Sofia's heart pounds.
The plain clothes cops move toward it.
The car speeds up. Keeps going.
10:47 PM.
Nothing explodes.
10:48 PM.
Still nothing.
10:49 PM.
Sofia starts breathing again.
SOFIA (V.O.)
Maybe... maybe that's all it takes. Not violence. Not
secrets. Not trying to save everyone alone. Just... truth.
Just asking for help. Just trusting people to be better
than they think they can be.
She stands up.
Walks over to where her dad and Jorge are sitting, talking
quietly.
                    SOFIA
          Tío?
                    JORGE
          Yeah?
                    SOFIA
          Where are you going to go?
                    JORGE
               (shrugs)
          Witness protection. They say they
          can help. I'll have to leave.
          Change my name. Start over. Alone.
                    SOFIA
          Or...
They both look at her.
                    SOFIA
          Or we all go. As a family. Start
          over. Together.
                    RAMÓN
          Mija, that's crazy--
                    SOFIA
          Is it? More crazy than staying
          here and waiting? More crazy than
          splitting up? We're a family.
          Families stay together. Even when
          it's hard. Especially when it's
          hard.
Silence.
And then--
Abuela walks over. Puts her hand on Jorge's shoulder.
                    ABUELA

                    She's right. We go together. Or we
                    don't go at all.
SOFIA (V.O.)
I don't know if this is the solution. I don't know if the
loop is finally broken. But for the first time in fifteen
times, I'm not trying to hold everyone together. I'm
letting them hold each other. Letting them hold me.
She closes her eyes.
SOFIA (V.O.)
Please. Please let this be enough. Please let me wake up
somewhere else. Some other day. Any other day.
                                                    FADE TO BLACK.
                          SMASH CUT TO
INT. SOFIA'S BEDROOM - MORNING (8:47 AM)

Sofia wakes. Sits up. Stares at nothing.

SOFIA (V.O.)
I told them the truth.
The cops came. Uncle Jorge left with
witness protection. And we all woke
up here again. Because the problem
isn't the gang. Isn't the explosion.
Isn't even Uncle Jorge.

She stands. Walks to her window.

SOFIA (V.O.) (CONT'D)
The problem is me. I'm the constant.
The lightning wants me. It's always
wanted me. So maybe... maybe if I'm
not here...

EXT. BUS STATION - MORNING (9:30 AM)

Sofia stands at the Greyhound counter. Small backpack. Cash
in hand.

                    TICKET AGENT
          Where to?

                    SOFIA
          Anywhere. Farthest you can get me
for two hundred dollars.

                    TICKET AGENT
          That'd be... Portland. Leaves in
twenty minutes.

Sofia nods. Takes the ticket.

EXT. BUS STATION PLATFORM - CONTINUOUS

Sofia sits on a bench. Waiting. Her phone buzzes
constantly.
She doesn't look at it.

SOFIA (V.O.)
If I'm not there, the lightning
can't find me. If the lightning
can't find me, my family is safe.
Simple math. I remove myself from
the equation.

Her phone: ABUELA calling.

Sofia stares at it. Lets it ring.

SOFIA (V.O.) (CONT'D)
They'll be sad. They'll wonder where
I went. But they'll be alive. And
that's what matters.

The bus pulls up. Door opens.

Sofia stands. Walks toward it.

ABUELA (O.S.)
Mija.

Sofia freezes.

She turns.

Abuela stands there. Somehow. Impossibly. She shouldn't
know
Sofia is here.

                    ABUELA (CONT'D)
          Running from lightning is like
running from your shadow.

                    SOFIA
          How did you--

                    ABUELA
          I know things. I've always known
things. Your mother knew too.

She walks closer.

                    ABUELA (CONT'D)
          You think this is about protecting
us. But lightning doesn't strike
to destroy, mija. It strikes to
transform.

                         SOFIA
               I've died sixteen times, Abuela.
Sixteen. I'm tired.

                         ABUELA
               Then stop running. Stop dying.
Start choosing.

                         SOFIA
               Choosing what?

                         ABUELA
               To live. Really live. For
               yourself.
Not for us.

The bus driver honks.

                       BUS DRIVER
               Lady, you coming or what?

Sofia looks at the bus. At her grandmother. At her ticket.

SOFIA (V.O.)
She's right. I've been trying to
save everyone else. Sacrifice
myself over and over. But that's
just another kind of death.

She tears the ticket in half.

                         SOFIA
               Take me home.

Abuela smiles. Takes her hand.

EXT. RODRIGUEZ HOUSE - NOON (12:00 PM)

Sofia stands in the driveway. The party is setting up. Her
family moving around. Alive. Unaware.

She takes a deep breath.

SOFIA (V.O.)
This time I'm not running. Not
sacrificing. Not trying to save
anyone. This time I choose me.

She walks toward the backyard.

12:15 PM on her phone.

Then 12:25.

Then 12:33.

The sky darkens. Right on schedule.

Ball lightning forms.

Sofia stands in the center of the yard.

                    SOFIA
               (loud, clear)
          Everyone get inside. Now.

Her family looks at her. At the sky. At the lightning
forming.

They run inside.

Only Mateo hesitates.

                    MATEO
          Sofia, what are you--

                    SOFIA
          Trust me. Please.

He nods. Runs inside.

Sofia alone in the yard.

The ball lightning descends.

She doesn't run. Doesn't hide. Doesn't try to protect
anyone
else.

She just stands there.

                    SOFIA (CONT'D)
          I'm ready.

The lightning reaches her.

But this time--

She doesn't touch it.

She ACCEPTS it.

There's a difference.

BRILLIANT LIGHT.

DARKNESS.

INT. SOFIA'S BEDROOM - MORNING (8:47 AM)

Sofia's eyes open.

Different this time.

She knows what she has to do.

> SOFIA
> She gets up. Certainty in every
> movement.

> SOFIA (CONT'D)
> I choose me.

FADE IN:
INT. SOFIA'S BEDROOM - MORNING - 8:47 AM
Sofia's eyes open. Different this time. No panic. No dread.
She sits up slowly, looks at her hands. Studies them like
she's seeing them for the first time.
The morning light cuts through her curtains at the same
angle as always. But everything feels changed.

> SOFIA
> (to herself, quiet)
> Okay.

She stands. Walks to her mirror. Looks at herself - really
looks.

> SOFIA
> I choose me.

A beat. She nods to herself.
INT. KITCHEN - CONTINUOUS
Abuela stands at the stove, stirring something. Sofia
enters.

> ABUELA
> Buenos días, mi estrella. How did
> you--

> SOFIA
> Abuela, I love you. But I can't
> take care of everyone today.

Abuela turns, wooden spoon in hand. Confused.

> ABUELA
> Mija?

> SOFIA
> I mean it. I love you so much. But
> today I need to take care of
> myself first.

A long beat. Abuela studies her granddaughter's face.

> ABUELA
> (soft)
> You sound different.

> SOFIA
> I am different.

Ramon enters, coffee mug in hand, work clothes already
dirty.

                    RAMON
          Morning. Sofia, can you--
                    SOFIA
          Dad. I'm going to community
          college. Starting next week. I
          need you to support that.
Ramon freezes mid-step. Coffee cup halfway to his lips.
                    RAMON
          What? Since when--
                    SOFIA
          Since always. I've been hiding it
          because I was scared you'd need me
          here. But I need this. I need my
          own life.
Ramon sets his cup down slowly. Something in Sofia's voice
- steel underneath the softness - stops him from arguing.
                    RAMON
              (after a long beat)
          Okay.
                    SOFIA
          Okay?
                    RAMON
              (clearing throat)
          Okay... we'll figure it out.
Sofia's eyes water. She wasn't expecting it to be this
simple.
                    SOFIA
          Thank you.
She kisses his cheek. Leaves him standing there, stunned.
EXT. BACKYARD - LATE MORNING - 11:00 AM
The party is already setting up. Mateo arranges folding
chairs. Uncle Jorge's truck is in the driveway.
Sofia watches from the back door. Takes a breath.
INT. LIVING ROOM - CONTINUOUS
Jorge sits on the couch, uncomfortable. Ramon putters in
the kitchen, visible through the doorway. Tension thick
enough to cut.
Sofia enters. Doesn't sit. Doesn't smooth things over.
                    SOFIA
          I'm going to let you two talk.
                    RAMON
          Sofia, you don't have to--
                    SOFIA
              (firm but kind)
          Yeah. I do have to. I have to not
          be in the middle anymore.
She walks to the kitchen door.
                    SOFIA
          Dad. He's your brother. I love you
          both. But this is between you two.
She leaves.
Jorge and Ramon sit in uncomfortable silence.

Finally:
>   RAMON
>   (not looking at Jorge)
>   You should have called.
>   JORGE
>   You're right.
>   RAMON
>   About... about Maria. You should
>   have--
>   JORGE
>   I know. I'm sorry.

Beat.

>   RAMON
>   I'm still angry at you.
>   JORGE
>   I know. I'm angry at me too.

They sit. Not comfortable. But real.

>   RAMON
>   (quieter)
>   She wouldn't have even been
>   driving if you hadn't--
>   JORGE
>   I know. I live with that every
>   day, hermano. Every single day.

Silence. Not resolution. But a start.

EXT. BACKYARD - 11:30 AM

Sofia finds Mateo setting up the grill.

>   MATEO
>   Hey! Happy birthday. Again. I
>   mean-- well, for me it's the first
>   time but--
>   SOFIA
>   Mateo.

He stops. Looks at her.

>   MATEO
>   Yeah?
>   SOFIA
>   I need your help today. At 12:30,
>   I need you to trust me. Whatever I
>   do, whatever I say - just trust
>   me.
>   MATEO
>   (concerned)
>   What's going to happen?
>   SOFIA
>   Something impossible. Something
>   magical. But I need to know you're
>   with me.

He searches her face. Sees something there he hasn't seen
before. Certainty.

>   MATEO
>   I'm always with you.

She takes his hand. Squeezes it.

>   SOFIA

                    Thank you. For believing me. Even
                    when it sounds crazy.
                              MATEO
                         (small smile)
                    Especially when it sounds crazy.
EXT. BACKYARD - 11:45 AM
More guests arrive. Music plays. Abuela directs people to
tables.
Danny arrives. Hands in pockets. Nervous.
Sofia walks directly to him. Pulls him aside by the fence.
                              DANNY
                    Hey Sofia, happy birth--
                              SOFIA
                    You brought a gun.
His face goes white.
                              DANNY
                    What? No, I--
                              SOFIA
                    Danny. Listen to me. People die
                    today if you don't give me that
                    gun right now.
                              DANNY
                    How did you--
                              SOFIA
                         (absolute certainty)
                    Give. It. To. Me.
Something in her voice - ancient and powerful - cuts
through his fear.
He reaches slowly into his waistband. Pulls out the
handgun. Hands it to her like it's burning his hand.
                              DANNY
                         (quiet, relieved)
                    I didn't want it anyway. They made
                    me-- those guys, they said--
                              SOFIA
                    I know. It's okay. You're safe
                    now.
She walks over to Officer Garcia, who's chatting with other
guests.
                              SOFIA
                    Garcia. I need you to hold onto
                    this until after the party. Can
                    you do that?
She hands him the gun.
Garcia's eyes go wide.
                         OFFICER GARCIA
                    Sofia, where did you--
                              SOFIA
                    It's handled. Just keep it safe.
                    Please.
He nods, secures it. Watches her walk away with new
respect.
EXT. STREET / FENCE LINE - 12:20 PM

Three young men approach the fence. Tattoos visible. Eyes
scanning the party.
They stop at the gate. Looking for someone.
Sofia sees them. Walks over calmly.
Guests notice. Music continues but people watch.

                    GANG MEMBER #1
          Yo. We're looking for Danny.
                    SOFIA
          He's not involved anymore. He's
          out.
                    GANG MEMBER #2
               (laughs)
          That's not how this works, mami.
                    SOFIA
          Yeah. It is.
She doesn't move. Doesn't flinch.
                    GANG MEMBER #1
               (harder)
          You don't understand--
                    SOFIA
          No. You don't understand. I'm not
          afraid of you. Not even a little.
Officer Garcia steps up behind her. Hand resting on his
belt.

                    OFFICER GARCIA
          And I'm SFPD. Off duty, but still
          SFPD. So I'd suggest you take the
          walk.
Standoff.
The gang members look at each other. At Sofia. At Garcia.
                    GANG MEMBER #1
               (backing away)
          Whatever. This ain't worth it.
They leave.
Mateo rushes to Sofia's side.
                    MATEO
          Are you okay?
                    SOFIA
               (breathing)
          Yeah. I'm good. I'm really good
          actually.
She checks her phone: 12:28 PM.
                    SOFIA
               (louder, to the party)
          Everyone! I need you to listen for
          a minute!
Conversations stop. Music quiets. Everyone turns.
Ramon stands by the grill. Jorge near the drinks. Abuela in
her chair. Anita with friends. Mateo beside Sofia.
                    SOFIA
          I know this is weird. But in about
          four minutes, something is going
          to happen. Something... magical.
Confused murmurs. Worried looks.

                              RAMON
                    Sofia, are you feeling okay?
                              ABUELA
                         (standing)
                    Let her speak.
          Sofia looks at her grandmother. Grateful.
                              SOFIA
                    I was born at 12:34 PM. Eighteen
                    years ago today. In the middle of
                    a lightning storm. Ball lightning
                    struck the hospital when I was
                    born.
                              ANITA
                         (to a friend)
                    Is she having a breakdown?
                              SOFIA
                    I've lived this day over and over.
                    Sixteen times. And I finally
                    understand what I'm supposed to
                    do.
                              MATEO
                         (quiet, to her)
                    I believe you.
          She squeezes his hand without looking at him.
                              SOFIA
                    The lightning isn't trying to kill
                    me. It's trying to give me a
                    choice.
                              JORGE
                    A choice about what?
          Sofia looks around at her family. Really sees them. All of
          them. Flawed. Beautiful. Hers.
                              SOFIA
                    About whether to keep sacrificing
                    myself to hold you all together...
                    or to let go. To trust that you'll
                    be okay. That I can love you AND
                    have my own life.
          12:32 PM on someone's watch.
          The sky begins to change.
          Clouds roll in - impossibly fast. Unnatural.
                              RAMON
                    What the--
          Thunder. Distant but coming closer.
          The wind picks up. Papers fly. Napkins scatter.
          Guests look up. Concerned. Confused.
                              ANITA
                    What's happening?
                              SOFIA
                         (calm)
                    Don't be afraid. This is meant to
                    happen.
          12:33 PM.

The sky darkens further. Purple-green clouds. Lightning
flashing between them.
And then--
It appears.
BALL LIGHTNING.
Forming in mid-air above the backyard. The size of a small
car. Crackling with impossible colors - blues and purples
and whites that shouldn't exist together.
Guests scream. Some run toward the house.

                         RAMON
          Sofia! Get away from it!
But Sofia doesn't move. She stands her ground.
The lightning descends slowly. Deliberately. Moving toward
her.

                         ABUELA
                  (crying)
          Dios mío...
Sofia raises her hand.

                         SOFIA
          I know what you want.
The lightning pulses brighter. A sound - not words exactly,
but understanding floods Sofia's mind.
VOICE (O.S.)

                    WHAT DO YOU CHOOSE?
          SOFIA
I choose me. I choose my life. My dreams. My future.
The lightning shifts. Tendrils point toward her family,
huddled near the house.
VOICE (O.S.)

                    WHAT ABOUT THEM?
          SOFIA
I love them. So much. But I'm not responsible for their
choices anymore. Only mine.
The sphere rotates slowly. Considering.
VOICE (O.S.)
YOU WERE MARKED TO BE ESPECIAL Y IMPORTANTE.
                         SOFIA
          I AM special. I AM important. Not
          because I sacrifice myself.
          Because I'm me. Because I exist.
          Because I choose to live.
The lightning begins to open. Unfurling like a flower
blooming.
Inside the light: images. Visions.
Multiple timelines. Infinite possibilities. Sofia sees
herself - helping people, using some gift she doesn't
understand yet, living fully, thriving, free.
But in every vision where she succeeds, she's chosen
herself first.
In every vision where she sacrifices, she's trapped.
Diminished. Lost.
And there - her mother's face. Maria. Young. Healthy.
Smiling.
                    MARIA'S VOICE

                    (echoing, warm)
          Let go, mija. I'm always with you.
          Always.
Tears stream down Sofia's face.
                    SOFIA
          Mom...
VOICE (O.S.)
                    WILL YOU ACCEPT YOUR GIFT?
          Sofia looks at the lightning. At
          the visions. At the impossible
          choice being offered.
She looks back at her family. At Mateo. At Abuela.
Then back to the lightning.
                    SOFIA
          Yes. I accept.
She reaches out with both hands.
Touches the ball of lightning.
BRILLIANT WHITE LIGHT explodes outward--
Sofia is lifted off the ground. Arms spread. Head back.
                    FAMILY
                (screaming)
                    SOFIA!
          Energy surges through her.
          Visible. Electric. Her body glows.
Her feet are two feet off the grass. Hair floating. Eyes
white light.
The backyard is bathed in blinding radiance.
Time seems to stop.
Everyone frozen in that moment. Watching. Unable to look
away despite the brightness.
Then--
The light begins to fade.
Gently. Softly.
Sofia lowers back to the ground. Feet touching grass.
The ball lightning dissipates into thousands of tiny
sparkles that drift upward like fireflies.
Sofia stands. Steady. Whole.
She's glowing slightly - then it fades completely.
She opens her eyes. They're normal again. But something in
them has changed. Ancient. Aware. Powerful.
Someone's phone: 12:35 PM.
Total silence.
Just wind. Birds. The world returning.
Sofia turns to her family.
                    SOFIA
          I'm okay.
Abuela rushes to her. Crying. Embracing her.
                    ABUELA
          I told you. Especial y importante.
          I told you!
Ramon runs over. Hugs them both.
                    RAMON
          What just-- what was-- are you--
                    SOFIA

                    (laughing through tears)
          I'm okay, Dad. I'm better than
          okay. I made the right choice.
Mateo approaches slowly. Cautious. Amazed.
                    MATEO
          You were... you were floating.
          Your eyes were--
She takes his hand.
                    SOFIA
          I know. I saw everything, Mateo.
          Everything I could be. Everything
          we could be.
He pulls her into a hug. Holds her tight.
The party slowly, carefully resumes. People in shock but...
celebrating.
Because sometimes magic happens. And sometimes people
witness it.
INT. BACK PORCH - EVENING - DUSK
Sofia sits on the porch steps. Exhausted but peaceful.
Abuela comes out. Sits beside her. Hands her a plate of
food.
                    ABUELA
          Eat, mija. You need strength after
          all that.
Sofia takes the plate. Picks at it.
                    SOFIA
          Why didn't you tell me more? About
          what I was? What I could become?
                    ABUELA
          Because you had to find out for
          yourself. Just like your mother
          knew you would.
Sofia looks at her.
                    SOFIA
          She knew?
                    ABUELA
          Before she died, she made me
          promise. She said: "Let Sofia
          choose her own path. Don't hold
          her back out of fear." She knew
          you were marked for something
          special.
Tears fall down Sofia's face.
                    SOFIA
          I miss her so much.
                    ABUELA
                    (taking her hand)
          She's always with you, mija. In
          the lightning. In your courage. In
          your choice today.
They sit in silence. Comfortable.
                    ABUELA
          So. Community college?
                    SOFIA

         (laughing)
    Yeah. Starting next week.
          ABUELA
    Good. You should have told us
    sooner.
          SOFIA
    I was afraid. Afraid everything
    would fall apart without me
    holding it together.
          ABUELA
    And look - we're still here. Your
    father and Jorge are talking
    inside like actual adults. Anita
    broke up with that boy. We're
    okay.
Sofia leans her head on Abuela's shoulder.
          SOFIA
    We're okay.
INT. SOFIA'S ROOM - NIGHT - 10:00 PM
Sofia lies on her bed. Door open. Mateo sits at her desk
chair.
          MATEO
    So... you're magic?
          SOFIA
         (laughing)
    I guess? I don't fully understand
    it yet. But yeah. Something like
    that.
          MATEO
    And you're going to community
    college?
          SOFIA
    Yeah. English and Education. Maybe
    become a teacher.
          MATEO
    Good. You should. You deserve it.
They sit in comfortable silence.
          MATEO
    Thank you for trusting me today.
    For letting me be there.
          SOFIA
    Thank you for believing me. Even
    when it sounded impossible.
          MATEO
    Always. I'll always believe you.
He stands. Kisses her forehead.
          MATEO
    Happy birthday, Sofia.
          SOFIA
    Best one yet.
He leaves. Sofia lies there. Smiling.
She closes her eyes.
INT. SOFIA'S BEDROOM - NEXT MORNING - 7:15 AM
Sofia's eyes open.

Different light through her curtains.
She grabs her phone: Wednesday, June 19th. 7:15 AM.
The next day. Actually the next day.
She sits up. Laughs. Cries. Both at once.
Abuela appears in her doorway.

> ABUELA
> Buenos días, mija.

Sofia jumps up. Runs to her. Hugs her tight.

> SOFIA
> It's tomorrow! It's actually
> tomorrow!

> ABUELA
> Sí. Tomorrow came. Just like you
> made it come.

> SOFIA
> I did it. I actually did it.

> ABUELA
> I never doubted you.

They stand in the doorway. Holding each other. The morning
sun warm on their faces.

                                        FADE TO:

                        EPILOGUE
EXT. COMMUNITY COLLEGE CAMPUS - ONE WEEK LATER - MORNING
Sofia walks across campus. Backpack on. Notebook in hand.
Nervous but excited.
Students everywhere. Talking. Laughing. Living their lives.
She takes a deep breath. Smiles.
Her phone rings. She answers.

> SOFIA
> Hola, Abuela.

                        INTERCUT:
INT. FAMILY HOUSE - KITCHEN - SAME TIME
Abuela at the kitchen table. Coffee. Sunlight.

> ABUELA
> How is your first day, mi
> estrella?

> SOFIA
> It's good. Really good. I'm about
> to go into English class.

> ABUELA
> We're so proud of you.

> SOFIA
> How's everyone? Dad? Jorge?

> ABUELA
> Your father fixed the fence
> yesterday. Jorge went to his
> meeting - three weeks now, still
> going strong. Anita is actually
> doing her homework without anyone
> telling her to.

Sofia laughs.

> SOFIA
> See? Everyone's okay.

                         ABUELA
          They were always going to be okay,
          mija. They just needed to learn
          they could be. And so did you.
                         SOFIA
          I love you, Abuela.
                         ABUELA
          Te amo, mi estrella. Now go. Go
          learn something.
                         SOFIA
          I will.
She hangs up. Stands outside her classroom building.
Students stream past her. Into their futures.
Sofia looks up at the sky.
Clear. Blue. Beautiful.
But for just a second - barely there - she sees it.
A flicker of ball lightning. Distant. Barely visible.
Benevolent.
Watching over her like a guardian.
Sofia smiles. Nods toward it.
The flicker disappears.
She adjusts her backpack. Takes one more breath.
Then walks toward her classroom. Toward her future.
Ready for whatever comes next.
INT. CLASSROOM - CONTINUOUS
Sofia enters. Finds a seat by the window.
Other students settling in. Professor at the front
organizing notes.
Sofia opens her notebook. Writes at the top of the first
page:
"Sofia Rodriguez - English 101"
Then underneath, smaller:
"Day One"
She looks out the window one more time. Sky still clear.
She smiles to herself.
Turns her attention to the front of the class.
The professor begins.
                         PROFESSOR
          Welcome to English 101. This
          semester we're going to explore
          the power of storytelling...
Sofia writes. Listens. Learns.
The camera slowly PULLS BACK through the window.
Past Sofia at her desk. Past the classroom. Out into the
open sky.
The sun shines. Birds fly. The world turns.
And Sofia Rodriguez - marked by lightning, freed by choice
- begins her next chapter.
                                        FADE OUT.

THE END.